READ ALL OF
AXEL & BEAST'S
ADVENTURES!

ANTARCTIC ATTACK

ADRIAN C. BOTT ART BY ANDY ISAAC

Kane Miller
A DIVISION OF EDC PUBLISHING

First American Edition 2017
Kane Miller, A Division of EDC Publishing

Text Copyright © Adrian C Bott 2016
Illustration Copyright © Andy Isaac 2016
First published in Australia by Hardie Grant Egmont 2016

For information contact:
Kane Miller, A Division of EDC Publishing
P.O. Box 470663
Tulsa, OK 74147-0663
www.kanemiller.com
www.edcpub.com
www.usbornebooksandmore.com

Library of Congress Control Number: 2016955652

Manufactured by Regent Publishing Services, Hong Kong
Printed May 2017 in ShenZhen, Guangdong, China

1 2 3 4 5 6 7 8 9 10

ISBN: 978-1-61067-704-2

CHAPTER 1

There's nothing quite like having a **secret den.** Whether it's a tree house, a basement or just a private place of your own, it's good to have somewhere you can unwind and be yourself.

Axel's secret den was very unusual. It was a cave dug out of the earth below his house.

There were two ways you could get into the secret lair. Either you could go down the steps into the cellar of the house and walk through the large **robot-shaped hole** that had been smashed through the wall, or from the backyard, you could press a button on a remote control and part of the lawn would fold away, revealing the cave below.

Most boys wouldn't have been able to make a den like that, but then most boys didn't have a shape-shifting robot for a friend. And Axel did.

The robot's name was **BEAST.** He was a runaway, hiding in Axel's house. Right now he was playing ping-pong with Axel. The paddle looked ridiculously tiny in his huge robot fist.

BEAST had a sad history. A greedy, evil company called **Grabbem Industries** had built him. He was supposed to be a super-powered suit of armor that would let young

Gus Grabbem Junior help his father smash things up; but when BEAST found out that the things he was meant to be smashing up were things he loved, such as plants, animals and ... well ... most of nature, he decided to get out.

Now Axel and BEAST were a team. They worked together to fight Grabbem Industries, and anyone else who threatened the planet.

Over the weeks since BEAST had crashed into his life, Axel had equipped his secret den with all sorts of **cool stuff.** It really helped that his mom, Nedra, was good friends with Rusty Rosie, who ran a junkyard. That meant Axel could get lots of secondhand items that just needed a bit of fixing up. It also meant some welcome company for Nedra, who'd been lonely since Axel's dad had mysteriously disappeared the year before.

The den had a refrigerator, a sofa, most of a weight machine, an exercise bike, a desktop computer, a pool table, a ping-pong table and an enormous TV. For some reason, the TV had a **moustache** permanently glued to the middle of the screen, which meant that almost everyone who appeared on it got a moustache.

Axel was sweating as he smacked the ping-pong ball back and forth.

Playing against BEAST was like playing a video game with the difficulty set to max. His robot reflexes were astoundingly quick. But there was a problem. BEAST didn't seem to want to **win.** He never took advantage of Axel's mistakes. So usually they just ended up batting the ball between them until Axel got tired.

"Arrrr!" Axel yelled suddenly, and slammed the ball as hard as he could.

It shot past BEAST's head, rebounded off the cave wall and vanished under the refrigerator. BEAST watched it go, turned back to Axel and blinked his luminous eyes.

"YOU ARE ANGRY," he said.

"Yeah," said Axel. He flung himself onto the sofa. "Not at you, though," he quickly added, before BEAST began to fret (which he often did). "I'm just tired of being cooped up in here with nothing to do."

BEAST tilted his head. "BUT WE HAVE FUN TOGETHER."

Axel sighed. "I know. But we haven't heard from Agent Omega for *ages*! Think how much fun we could have if you had a new set of apps!"

BEAST's apps were what let him change form into new shapes with new powers. Their mysterious friend Agent Omega had promised them a new set of apps with each mission to fight Grabbem Industries, but so far they had only been sent on one. At least he'd sent them some experimental apps to test out in the meantime.

Just then, the gong went. **CLANG!!** Axel had left an old dinner gong next to the cellar entrance, because there was no door to knock on.

"Come in!" he yelled.

Nedra came in, carrying some cans of soda. She set them down on the big wooden cable spool that Axel used for a table. "Break time," she said.

"Thanks, Mom!"

Behind her came Rusty Rosie, who looked around at the secret lair and grinned. "Wow. This place is really coming along, mate!"

"I guess," Axel said. "Mom, I was thinking...

we haven't seen any sign of Grabbem for ages, so I thought maybe BEAST and I could, well, you know …"

"You want to go out on a **joyride,** don't you?" said Nedra. Her eyes narrowed. "Axel, we've been over and over this. BEAST isn't a toy."

"But I never get any practice with him!" Axel groaned. "We're supposed to be a team. All we ever do down here is play games, mess around and wait for a call that never comes!"

Nedra sat down next to him. "I know it's frustrating. But Agent Omega was very clear. **'Stay out of sight,'** he said. **'Keep your heads down.'** So that's what we have to do."

Axel glanced at the silent computer across the cave. "I wish he'd call. It's been so long. What if they've caught him?" Agent Omega was a double agent within Grabbem's ranks.

"If they had, they'd be coming after us next," Nedra said. "All the more reason to stay hidden."

Axel picked up a can of soda. He felt like one himself – one that had been shaken up until it was on the verge of bursting. He popped it open. With a **hisssss,** foam erupted out of the can and spurted onto the ground. *Great.*

"Couldn't they just run around the house a few times?" Rosie suggested.

Nedra folded her arms. "Not happening."

Rosie shrugged. "You're the responsible adult. Your call. I'll say this, though. I don't know about BEAST, but young Axel here is going to go **stir-crazy** if he doesn't get out soon, and that's a fact."

Axel gazed at BEAST, remembering how good it felt to climb inside the robot's padded chest and wear him like a power suit of armor. When that happened, he was no longer a skinny boy who needed strong glasses and hid from bullies in the school supply closet. He was *powerful*. He could fly, lift trucks, and even shoot beams of energy, if the right app was installed ...

Boop-de-doop, sang the computer suddenly. **Beep-boop-dee.**

Axel's eyes widened.

"It's him," he yelled. "It's Agent Omega. He's finally calling!"

CHAPTER 2

Axel dived across the room and clicked on **accept incoming call.**

For a second there was silence, and he thought he must have been too late. But then the screen changed and showed a grainy image of Agent Omega hunched in front of his own computer.

"Where have you been?" Axel burst out.

"Keeping my head down," Agent Omega

said, "and I hope you've been doing the same."

"Oh, he has," interrupted Nedra. "I've made sure of that."

Agent Omega peered at his screen. "Looks like you've been hard at work. Nice lair you've built. Is that a pool table? Maybe we can have a game sometime. Anyway, I'll get right to the point. I have a mission for you."

"Yes!" Axel punched the air.

"You might not feel that way once you've found out where you're going," Agent Omega warned. "You'll want to dress warm. I'm sending you to **Antarctica.**"

"Antarctica!" Axel echoed. "That means snow, ice …"

"Seals," said Nedra.

"Whales," said Rosie.

"AND PENGUINS!" said BEAST happily.

"Yes, all of those," said Agent Omega, "and one other thing. Oil. I'm certain that's what Grabbem are after. Axel, take a look at these pictures. You, uh, might want to get BEAST to look the other way. They're pretty upsetting."

Axel turned around, but BEAST had already heard and had begun playing a game of pool with himself, **humming softly** all the while.

"Animals have been found covered in oil in the extreme south," said Agent Omega.

Axel's screen flashed an image of a penguin covered head to foot in **filthy sludge.** The next image: dead fish floating in an oil slick. The next, a baby seal streaked with black stains.

"You don't have to show me any more. I get the idea," said Axel. He felt sickened and angry. Grabbem were going to pay for this.

"I just want you to know what's at stake. Grabbem have been running an operation in Antarctica for some time now, and they've been doing it in secret. **They're sneaky.**"

"Why would Grabbem go after oil in the Antarctic?" asked Nedra. "Sure, there's meant to be oil there, but isn't it too hard to get to, because of the ice sheet in the way?"

"That's where **the Devastator** comes in."

Axel felt a chill. "The Devastator? Sounds scary."

"It is. From what I can tell, it's a gigantic vehicle with some kind of huge gun, or drill. Grabbem are going to use it to punch right through the ice to the oil beneath. It has to be charged up before use, and it'll be ready in twelve hours."

Twelve hours to save Antarctica, thought

Axel. "I'm in," he said. "What do you need us to do?"

Agent Omega typed rapidly. "I'm sending BEAST the coordinates for the region where the most pollution was found. The Grabbem base must be somewhere within that area. You'll have to search for it."

"And the Devastator?"

"If you can find the Grabbem base in time, we can shut this operation down before the Devastator is fully charged."

"Just one more thing …"

"You need **apps,**" Agent Omega said, "and oh boy, do I have a set of **apps** for you!"

BEAST stood up suddenly from his solitary game of pool. **"RECEIVING DATA,"** he said, sounding as happy as a toddler who's just heard the ice cream truck coming.

"The apps you can have for this mission are **SKYHAWK, SHARKOS, SNOW-DOG, MYTHFIRE** and **LAZBOLT**," Agent Omega explained.

Behind Axel, Rosie whistled. "Sweet. I'm kind of jealous."

"I already know about SKYHAWK, SHARKOS and LAZBOLT," Axel said.

SKYHAWK was a jet-plane-like form that had no weapons, but could fly above the clouds at **mind-boggling** speeds. SHARKOS was BEAST's special underwater form, an armored submarine that could drop mines and **electrify** the water like an eel.

As for LAZBOLT, it was a laser blaster, one of the experimental apps Omega had sent for them to test. It couldn't move fast, but it put out a beam that could **slice** a tank in half as easily as unzipping a jacket. BEAST's forms always took something away as well as adding something, so LAZBOLT gained firepower but lost speed.

"What do the others do?" Axel asked.

"Near as I can make out, SNOWDOG is some kind of snowmobile-like form equipped to handle icy conditions."

Axel nodded. "And MYTHFIRE?"

"No idea. I put that one in because it was marked as **super dangerous.** Figured you could use a little danger on your side."

"ELEVEN HOURS AND FIFTY-FIVE MINUTES UNTIL DEVASTATOR ACTIVE," said BEAST.

"Oh, and I programmed BEAST with a timer," added Agent Omega. "That's how long you've got before the Devastator comes online. Don't waste any time. Every second counts."

"Got it. And thanks."

"Good luck." With a quick salute, Agent Omega vanished.

Axel felt like he was walking on air. Finally, after all these weeks of bouncing off the walls, **a mission!** He went to open BEAST and climb inside, but the look on his mother's face stopped him. "What?"

"Stay and eat something. I don't want you racing off before you've had your lunch."

"But Mom! This is **urgent!**"

Nedra glared at him. "How are you going to protect the environment from Grabbem if you can't even look after yourself?"

Eleven hours and fifty-four minutes left, thought Axel. *And every second counts.*

"I'll be okay. I know I will!"

Nedra threw up her hands. "Fine, I give up. Go and save the world on an empty stomach! Come on, Rosie. Let's get out of here before the place fills up with rocket fumes."

The moment they left, Axel quickly opened the transparent panel on BEAST's chest and climbed inside. He pressed a control and the upper entrance to the secret lair slid open, letting in the daylight.

"Let's go, BEAST," he said.

CHAPTER 3

BEAST fired his thrusters. Together they rocketed upward, out of the secret lair and high into the sky above the house. After being stuck inside for so many long weeks, Axel finally felt the thrill of freedom.

"We need to get to Antarctica, fast. BEAST, shift form to **SKYHAWK.**"

BEAST's legs lengthened and his arms converted into the sleek wings of SKYHAWK, his jet-fighter form. His head became longer, more streamlined.

Axel braced himself. "Give me maximum thrust!"

With a **KA-BOOM!** of igniting jets, SKYHAWK tore through the sky.

Down on the ground, far below, people looked up in sudden confusion. What was a high-speed plane doing in this part of the country?

Now positioned on his stomach, Axel relaxed in the cockpit. Using the controls, he guided SKYHAWK steadily up and up until they plunged into the cloud barrier. Everything was lost in a world of white mist.

Moments later, they broke through above the clouds. The view took Axel's breath away.

When you are high enough up, there is no such thing as a rainy or overcast day. The weather, whatever it may be, only ever goes up as high as the cloud level. The sun is always shining above the clouds, and if you have a way of reaching them, you can prove it for yourself.

It was like entering a dream world. Brilliant sunlight lit up a realm of billowy, pillow-soft clouds. They looked almost solid enough to walk on, like a colossal **marshmallow** mattress reaching into infinity.

"How long till we reach Antarctica?" Axel asked.

"THREE HOURS."

"Whoa. Maybe I *should* have let my mom make lunch."

"BEAST HAS EMERGENCY FOOD SUPPLIES, IF YOU REQUIRE THEM." A little tube popped up in front of Axel's mouth.

Axel eyed it suspiciously. "This is food?"

"LIQUI-NUMS ARE NUTRITIOUS AND CONTAIN EVERYTHING YOU NEED TO SURVIVE!" BEAST chanted happily. "BEAST HAS ENOUGH FOR TWO WEEKS."

Axel had never heard of **Liqui-Nums.** They must be some Grabbem project. Probably one that never made it out of the research labs. He sucked experimentally on the tube.

Sludge flooded his mouth. It tasted as if a cherry had fallen into a bucket of wallpaper paste, done a **bubbly burp** and climbed out again.

LIQUI-NUMS!™

"When there's no time for taste!"

There was nowhere to spit it out inside BEAST's head, so Axel had to swallow it. "BEAST, that stuff is *gross*!"

"YOU ARE BEAST'S PILOT, AXEL. BEAST WILL NOT LET YOU STARVE."

"Better save the emergency food for real emergencies," said Axel, thinking, *It would have to be an emergency to make me eat THAT stuff.*

"How are we going to pass the time?"

Luckily, BEAST had an onboard movie player, so Axel was able to leave the flying up to BEAST and relax with some of his favorite cartoons. After that, they spent a half hour singing together, with BEAST **beatboxing** and Axel making up rap lyrics.

Then BEAST closed his canopy screens to make it dark so Axel could doze for a while, with BEAST carefully steering them on their way above the clouds.

Meanwhile, deep within Grabbem's secret Antarctic base, a boy called Gus Grabbem Junior was running down a steel-walled corridor. In his hand he held an electronic key labeled **"Devastator."** The ghoulish grin on his face meant he was looking forward to doing something very, very nasty. That grin would have made hardened headmasters shudder. It was the kind of grin you might see on a wolf who's just been given a job as a shepherd.

A chime rang. Axel woke up to find he'd **dribbled** on BEAST's comfortable padded lining. "Hmm? Wha–? Urrrr. Sorry, buddy. I guess I fell asleep."

"YOU HAVE BEEN ASLEEP FOR SEVENTY-SIX MINUTES," said BEAST.

Axel's stomach growled loudly.

"WOULD YOU LIKE SOME **LIQUI-NUMS?**"

"No! I mean, no thanks. Are we nearly there yet?"

"YES. THAT IS WHY I WOKE YOU."

"Better let me take over the controls so I can bring us down."

BEAST's internal displays lit up. Axel felt a shock as he saw that they were only a few feet above the sea, which was the intense blue color of a **bubblegum slushie** and looked about as warm. In the far distance was a lonely looking ship, a trawler of some kind.

"Geez, BEAST, we're flying a bit low, aren't we? Those fishermen might see us!"

"BEAST IS SORRY. OUR FLIGHT PATH IS QUITE SAFE. BEAST DID NOT MEAN TO SCARE YOU."

"It's okay. Let's take a look at Antarctica."

Up ahead, the sea came to an end and there began a great rolling plain of white, with patches of gray black showing through, and mountains like mounds of frosting in the distance. It looked pure, unspoiled and **lonely.** You could shout forever in those fields of blowing snow and nobody would hear you.

We're at the end of the world, thought Axel. *People aren't meant to live here. Just the creatures that already do.*

"What a view," Axel breathed. "Wait. Are those penguins?"

BEAST's tracking cameras zoomed in on the coastline. Sure enough, there was a group of penguins flocking together on the shore. **EMPERORS?** the display read.

Axel laughed with joy. "Look at them! They're amazing!"

And they were. Tall, somehow silly and noble at the same time, the penguins wobbled up and down the rocky beach. Some of them slid into the water to fish. Little gray chicks looked up at their parents and their mouths gaped, waiting for food. Axel wanted to climb out and play with them, but he knew they needed to be left to themselves.

These defenseless little guys are the ones at risk from Grabbem, he reminded himself. There was no sign of any oil, though, and the penguins didn't look troubled at all. In fact, there were no ships, no buildings, no tents … no sign at all that anyone had ever been here.

"This *is* where Agent Omega meant us to go, right?" he asked.

"THESE **EXACT** COORDINATES," said BEAST.

"Let's shift to standard form. It's less noisy than SKYHAWK. I need to get in closer for a better look, but I don't want to scare the penguins."

BEAST resumed his robot form as they hovered close to the beach. Axel still couldn't see anything unusual – just rocks, snow and lots of penguins. Maybe Agent Omega was wrong, and the area was completely desolate.

And then one of the penguins waddled away from the others. It stood **stiffly** for a moment, spreading its wings out in a strange way.

The next second it **shot up** into the air. Its beak stuck out like a spike and a plume of rocket exhaust roared out of its bottom.

"What ???" yelled Axel.

The penguin streaked through the air like a missile. It was heading straight at them …

CHAPTER 4

There was only one chance to get out of the penguin missile's path in time. Axel flung BEAST into a sideways roll.

As BEAST flipped over and over, Axel felt the Liqui-Nums **sloshing** around in his stomach, fighting to come back up. He swallowed hard and leveled BEAST off again.

"BEAST, track that penguin, fast! Where did it go?"

A distant **KA-THOOM!** in the sky behind them told him the answer. He checked the rear-view screen and saw white smoke blooming against the blue, flecked with fiery fragments.

Axel stared at it in disbelief. He'd watched nature documentaries before. Emperor penguins did some incredible things. They went on long marches to their ancestral breeding grounds, braving the elements and surviving against the odds. But no nature documentary had ever mentioned penguins **exploding** before.

"Okay. Things just got weird," he said. "Looks like Grabbem have been here after all. At least the other penguins are okay ... oh, *no!*"

The other penguins were **not** okay. They were *all* doing that same stiff-standing, wing-spreading wobble-on-the-spot that the first one had done. And there were hundreds of them all along the beach.

"BEAST, we need to leave now!"

"ENGAGING FULL THRUST," BEAST replied.

One by one, the **penguin missiles** took to the air. They flew toward BEAST in a black-and-white swarm, smoke spewing out behind them as if their tails were on fire. The entire sky seemed to be filled with them.

A penguin rushed right at them. Axel glimpsed two little red dots where its eyes should have been. BEAST flew up out of the way in time, but only just. The explosion shook Axel around in his pilot's compartment.

"We can't dodge this many," he gasped. "Only one thing for it. Shift into **SHARKOS.** We're heading for the sea."

"ROGER!"

BEAST's arms flattened out and shortened, turning into fins. A smooth dorsal fin rose from his back. His legs clamped together and extended tail flukes above and below.

SHARKOS couldn't fly, of course, so Axel and BEAST were now plunging out of the sky. Axel crossed his fingers and hoped he'd gotten the angle right, or they'd belly flop. SHARKOS dived gracefully into the water, sending up a spout like a fountain. Axel breathed out in relief.

Now they were in a watery world of streaming bubbles and huge, half-visible masses of ice. Axel saw the flashes and bangs of exploding penguins above, and was glad to be out of the firing line.

"They looked so **cute,**" he said miserably. "I still can't believe penguins tried to kill us."

"THEY ARE STILL TRYING," said BEAST.

"What? Show me!"

Ranks of penguin rockets were hopping up to the edge of the ice and plunging in. As soon as they entered the water, they **whooshed** through it like miniature torpedoes. Axel let out a yell of frustration. "Of course! Penguins are **aquatic!** We're not safe from them under the water. If anything, they're even *more* dangerous down here!"

As if to prove him right, the horde of penguin missiles curved like planes in formation flight, arranging themselves into a pointed V-shape and coming directly at them.

"THESE ARE PROBABLY NOT NATURAL PENGUINS, BUT **ROBOT REPLICAS**," said BEAST.

"You think?"

Axel fired up the turbines that propelled SHARKOS through the water. There was no way to outswim the penguin torpedoes, and electric pulses were too short-range. He'd just have to think of something else, fast.

SHARKOS was armed with **mines,** but they could drop only one at a time. There was no way to stop so many attackers with one mine. Unless …

"Find the nearest patch of sea ice and head for it," he told BEAST.

SHARKOS wrenched itself around and swam full tilt. The penguins veered around to follow.

Up ahead, Axel saw what looked like a bluish-gray wall. As they drew closer, he saw it was something like an upside-down mountain, its peak lost in the shadowy depths of the sea. It must be the underside of an iceberg – and there was much more ice under the surface than there was above.

"Get ready to drop a mine when I give the word."

"MINE ARMED."

With the penguins racing after them, Axel steered SHARKOS on a steep plunge under the iceberg. The craggy ice rushed by overhead. Axel waited until they were right under the iceberg's heart.

"Steady … okay, drop!"

A tiny sphere – the mine – flew out of SHARKOS's tail with a soft **ploop.** Axel boosted the turbines to maximum and roared away through the water.

The oncoming flock of robot penguins paid no attention to the mine. Their glowing red eyes were on SHARKOS. One of them brushed against the mine with a wing, and –

KA-BLAMMO!

An explosion tore through the water, shattering the underside of the iceberg. Three of the robot penguins were blasted to scraps of metal on the spot. The others were buffeted, but kept coming – only to run straight into the huge chunks of ice that came drifting down into their path.

The water was suddenly full of ice fragments and the penguins couldn't stop. They yelled electronic squawks as they smashed into the ice boulders, one after the other. Only one was still coming, rocketing out of the storm of debris.

Axel spun SHARKOS on the spot, twisting the flexible robot body around as if it was a real shark. He yelled, "Electric pulse, **now!**"

From between SHARKOS's jaws came a piercing **screaannnnggg**, like

a rock guitarist turning the volume up to eleven. A cone of electrical energy frazzled the water in front of them. The penguin missile shuddered and then blew itself to bits as the electric pulse overloaded it.

Axel fell back against the seat cushions, gasping. "Oh, man. That was *not* what I was expecting. Rocket penguins? Who came up with **that?**"

"YOU NEED TO RELAX," said BEAST. "I SHALL PLAY SOME SOOTHING SOUNDS SPECIALLY CHOSEN FOR OUR CURRENT SITUATION."

Sloshy wave noises began to play in Axel's ears. Then came the **strange, echoing cry** of a humpback whale.

Axel flinched. "Thanks, BEAST, but please don't. It makes me think you've sprung a leak."

In the silence, he gathered his thoughts. *Grabbem are definitely here. Those robot penguins must be sentinels, put there to keep any pesky intruders out. Nobody would spot that they weren't normal penguins until it was too late. So what are they protecting?*

"LIFE FORM APPROACHING," said BEAST.

"What? Did we miss one of the penguins?"

"NO. THIS IS SOMETHING ELSE."

"The Devastator?"

BEAST said nothing.

Axel held his breath. The "life form" BEAST had mentioned was coming at them through the water, a ghostly gray shape with dark eyes ...

CHAPTER 5

Axel watched the creature emerge from the darkness. There was something silvery in its mouth.

"Is it **another robot?** Can you scan it?"

"THE CREATURE IS NATURAL," said BEAST.

The creature swam closer and closer. It seemed curious, not angry or scared. It swam right up until it was nose to nose with them.

The thing in its mouth was a fish.

Axel stared at the sleek, inhuman face looking into his own.

"It's a **leopard seal**," he said in awe. "I've read about those. They're dangerous."

Even inside the armored safety of BEAST, Axel felt uneasy. The seal's body was thick and muscular.

As he watched, uncertain what he should do next, the seal opened its mouth. The dead fish floated between them. The seal's mouth yawned wide, and inside Axel saw two terrifying rows of **teeth** – huge, curved and sharp. This wasn't a cute, fluffy seal, but a **powerful predator.** In these waters, only the killer whale was more deadly.

This animal belongs here, Axel thought. *We don't. We're strangers in its hunting ground. It's trying to scare us off.*

"Don't make any sudden moves, BEAST. I think it might be getting ready to attack."

"SHE," Beast said softly.

"Huh?"

"NOT 'IT.' **SHE.**"

"You can tell?"

"SHE TOLD ME."

Axel's mouth fell open. "You can *speak* **seal?**"

The seal pushed her head forward, nudging the fish at them. It floated past BEAST's head. Then she swam after it, grabbed it and pushed it at them again.

"MY SHARKOS FORM CAN **SCAN THE BRAIN WAVES** OF AQUATIC CREATURES," BEAST explained. "THIS ALLOWS ME A LIMITED FORM OF COMMUNICATION."

"Wow. So what's she saying?"

"I BELIEVE SHE IS TRYING TO FEED ME HER FISH."

Axel was **dumbfounded.** How wrong could he have been? Here they were, far from home, strangers in this icy sea … and the leopard seal was trying to help them. She hadn't been getting ready to attack at all. "She thinks we're hungry," he said. His stomach **rumbled** again. He wondered how the seal could possibly know something like that.

"NO. SHE THINKS WE ARE BAD AT HUNTING."

Axel laughed. "What?"

BEAST paused, scanning the seal's mind.

"Well? What's she thinking?"

"SHE SAYS: EVEN A PUP SEAL WOULD HAVE KNOWN THAT THOSE WERE NOT REAL PENGUINS, AND YET WE ATTACKED THEM. CLEARLY WE ARE **USELESS HUNTERS** AND NEED HELP. BUT WE ARE NOT EVEN SMART EONUGH TO EAT A GOOD FISH WHEN IT IS BROUGHT TO US."

The seal had given up trying to feed BEAST the fish. Axel thought he saw a look of frustration on her face as she turned and began to swim away.

"You should talk to my mom, seal," he said. "You've got a lot in common." He sighed and rested his head on the seat cushion. "Maybe we *are* bad hunters, BEAST. There are thousands of square miles of Antarctica out there and we've got **no idea** where Grabbem's base is. Those robot penguins looked just like the real thing! If they're that clever, how are we supposed to find them?"

"EVEN A PUP SEAL WOULD HAVE KNOWN," repeated BEAST.

"So what can a baby seal do that we can't?" Axel pondered. "BEAST, follow her, please. We need to talk to her some more."

They kept a respectful distance from the leopard seal as they followed her along the coast. Axel wasn't sure this was sensible, but it was the only lead they had.

After about a mile of swimming, they reached a long ice shelf jutting out of the land. There were more seals here, and they swam up to look at the strange newcomer.

The leopard seal swam back to BEAST and **bonked** him on the head with her nose.

"SHE IS WARNING US NOT TO COME TOO CLOSE BECAUSE THE CUBS MIGHT BE SCARED."

"That's fine. I just want to know how she could tell the penguins weren't real."

"SHE SAYS THEY SMELLED **WRONG**."

Of course! Seals had an excellent sense of smell when they were out of the water. His excitement growing, Axel said, "Please ask her if she's smelled anything else like that lately … anything wrong, man-made."

BEAST was silent for a long time. Axel realized he had no idea how BEAST was asking the seal a question in the first place. Understanding them was one thing, but actually **talking to them** was something else. "SHE IS VERY UPSET. THE **SMELLY MACHINES** HAVE BEEN POISONING THE FISH. I HAVE TOLD HER THAT WE

ARE HERE TO STOP THEM, AND SHE IS GLAD."

"Smelly machines? That's got to be Grabbem. Can she show us where they are?"

"LOOK, AXEL. SHE ALREADY IS."

The seal was heaving herself out of the water and onto the ice shelf. Axel shifted BEAST back into his robot form, and they pulled themselves out after her. The ice shelf **creaked** ominously under their weight.

The seal shuffled herself along, leading them away from the sea and into the snowy landscape. They followed her around the side of a rocky mound that hid the land beyond from view.

That must be why Grabbem picked this place, thought Axel. *Passing ships wouldn't suspect a thing.*

They hadn't gone far when a mountainous

shape came into view across the snowfields.

"*Hrooooonk*," said the seal.

"I don't think I need you to translate that," Axel said. "That's where the smelly machines are. And that's where we're going next."

BEAST said **"THANK YOU"** to the seal, who harrumphed, sniffed the air and wriggled her shoulders before shuffling away again. Axel wondered what she might be saying. He waited for BEAST to translate. He didn't. The moments ticked by.

"Well, what did she say?"

"BEAST DOES NOT WANT TO TELL YOU."

Axel frowned. This was new. BEAST sometimes had his own private thoughts, but he'd never clammed up like this before.

"Come on, BEAST. You can tell me anything. You know that."

"YES. BEAST KNOWS. BUT THE SEAL WAS NOT SPEAKING TO BOTH OF US JUST THEN. ONLY TO BEAST."

"Oh." Axel hadn't expected that. "So it was personal."

"YES."

"That's fine. You can have secrets. I don't mind."

BEAST hissed softly and his body **sagged** a bit, as if he were sighing in relief.

Axel smiled to himself. "We've got some more traveling to do. Let's give this **SNOW-DOG** form of yours a try – ***oof!***"

The ***"oof!"*** came as BEAST fell forward onto all fours. His arms and legs folded like an origami trick, becoming triangular caterpillar tracks. Tiny spikes extended from each slat of the track, ready to get a strong grip on the ice.

Axel yelled in surprise as the entire pilot compartment rotated up and through BEAST's body, leaving him sitting on BEAST's back looking out over the featureless plain.

BEAST's antennae became two tall pointy ears. His face became long and **wolflike.** His eyes became searchlights, casting two bright cones of misty light over the ground ahead. The background hum of his power reactor changed to a low growling sound.

"SNOWDOG TRANSFORMATION COMPLETE."

"Cool. Let's get to that iceberg, fast. Looks like the sun's setting."

"IT IS. AND WE HAVE ONLY THREE HOURS UNTIL THE DEVASTATOR IS UNLEASHED."

"And we still don't know what it is." Axel squeezed the throttle. SNOWDOG's tracks

bit into the ice and they set off, picking up more and more speed as they went. "I guess we won't have to wait long to find out …"

Meanwhile, in a hangar deep inside the Grabbem base, Gus Grabbem Junior looked up at **the Devastator.** It was a towering giant of a vehicle, with a cylinder-shaped body and three long thin legs. On the underside of the cylinder was Gus's favorite part, the **blaster cannon.** Cables were plugged into it, throbbing with light.

Gus wore a black leather jacket and a T-shirt covered in printed **bullet holes.** The scientist next to him wore a white lab coat and an anxious expression.

"Can't you charge it up any quicker?" Gus

snapped. "I want to start shooting holes in the ice. And anything else that gets in my way."

"We're charging it as fast as we can," stammered the scientist.

"You'd better be." Gus stuck his finger deep into his left nostril and worked it around. There was **something** wedged up in there and he wanted to get it.

The scientist licked his dry lips. "I must say, we were all, um, very surprised when your father informed us that you were to be the pilot. We were expecting someone with, ah, a little more experience."

"Are you saying I'm not good enough?" Gus snarled.

"No!" squeaked the scientist. "It's just that the *cost* … that is, the Devastator is worth **billions,** and you do have a reputation for …"

"Well?"

"Um … for crashing. A lot."

Gus grabbed the scientist by the scruff of his white coat and lifted him until he was standing on tiptoe.

"My dad says I'm the best pilot in the whole company," Gus leered. The gum he was chewing didn't cover up the **stink** of his bad teeth. "His opinion matters. Yours isn't worth squat. Now go and get me a can of soda."

As the scientist scurried away, Gus looked longingly at the gigantic door that led out of the base. Soon he could drive **the Devastator** out and start blasting mammoth holes in the landscape. His palms itched; he couldn't wait. The Antarctic ice sheet would look like **Swiss cheese** once he was finished with it …

CHAPTER 6

Every time Axel got to try out one of BEAST's forms for the first time, he got as excited as a kid waking up on Christmas morning. You never knew quite what you were going to get.

No two forms ever felt the same; flying SKYHAWK, which tore through the clouds faster than the speed of sound, was completely different to flying BLACKBAT, which glided silently and stealthily above the Earth, invisible to all below.

All the forms had different tools and weapons, too. SHARKOS dropped mines and fired electric pulses, OGRE used its heavy fists and GOPHER its sharp digging claws.

SNOWDOG was noisy. Axel knew that much now. They roared across the open Antarctic plain, sounding like a squad of stunt motorbikes putting on a show. Did SNOWDOG have any weapons? Axel wondered. Hopefully they wouldn't need to find out.

"I HAVE SCANNED OUR SURROUND-INGS, AND I HAVE A SUGGESTION," said BEAST.

"Pull off some **sick jumps** while we're here?" grinned Axel. "Do some snowboarding?"

"WE HAVE BEEN TAKEN BY SURPRISE ONCE ALREADY. **I RECOMMEND STEALTH.**"

"BEAST, this new SNOWDOG form of yours is about as stealthy as a clown with a **chainsaw!** We can't waste time sneaking around. We need to get to that mountain fast, before the Devastator wakes up."

A blue arrow pinged on Axel's display, above a range of low hills to their left.

"IF WE GO SLOWLY THROUGH THESE VALLEYS, WE MAY REACH OUR DESTINATION UNDETECTED."

"No," Axel decided. "We're running out of time already. I want **more** speed, not less."

"AS YOU WISH." SNOWDOG's engine roared even louder.

Axel smiled in satisfaction. *I didn't spend weeks cooped up indoors just to take things* *slowly on this mission. It's time to **let rip.***

Axel only got to enjoy racing SNOWDOG at full speed for a few minutes before doubt set in and he realized how **reckless** he was being. They'd charged in headlong when they first came to Antarctica, and the penguin missiles had nearly drowned them. Maybe that should have been a lesson in taking things more cautiously?

The more he thought it over, the sillier he felt. This wasn't supposed to be a thrilling vacation. This was an **important mission,** and a lot was riding on it. The leopard seal, and thousands like her, were counting on him – not to mention all the other Antarctic wildlife that Grabbem's greed would endanger.

"Actually, maybe we should head for the hills after all," said Axel. "Can we take a detour?"

"IT IS TOO LATE FOR THAT."

BEAST sounded strangely ominous, like a vampire in a horror movie.

A red dot appeared on BEAST's scanner. Something was coming up behind them, and closing in fast. "Oh, no," Axel groaned. "Don't tell me the Devastator's out already!"

"GRABBEM VEHICLES APPROACHING."

"Vehicles? But I only see one dot ..."

Axel paused. Over the noise of SNOWDOG's engine he could hear the **whup-whup-whup** of rotor blades.

BEAST flashed up a rear view.

Coming up at them through the gathering darkness was a gleaming black helicopter, with a dazzling searchlight shining from its underbelly. It was carrying a snowmobile on a long cable. The rider, who was wearing some sort of thick, padded explorer's outfit, had a gold crash helmet on. As the snowmobile swayed below the chopper, the rider shook his fist at Axel.

The next second, an amplified voice rang out from the chopper:

"Attention, trespasser! You are driving stolen Grabbem property. Bring your vehicle to a complete stop and step out with your hands above your head!"

"Oh, for the love of ... not those two losers again!" Axel banged his head repeatedly on the cushions. "It's Alpha One and Alpha Gold."

Axel had already had one run-in with Alpha One and his younger brother, Alpha Gold. They were Grabbem pilots who were bent on capturing Axel and returning BEAST to the Grabbem factory where he was made. The last time their paths had crossed, Axel had defeated them – to their total embarrassment.

The Alpha boys somehow managed to keep their jobs no matter how badly they messed up. Axel wasn't sure why, but he expected it was because the pair of them were so eager to show off, they'd charge into any danger their boss told them to.

"Yahoo!" shouted Alpha Gold, who was sitting in the dangling snowmobile. "We've got them now for sure. Drop me as close as you can!"

Alpha One was in the chopper, and he was furious. "It isn't fair. Why'd I get stuck flying the chopper?"

"Because you lost the coin toss."

"It's supposed to be best of three!"

"Says who? Hey – stop *swinging me around!*"

"Sorry," smirked Alpha One as he lurched

the helicopter from side to side. "It's just **SOOOO** windy up here. I don't know if I can fly level."

"Aaaaarrr!"

The snowmobile swung back and forth like a pendulum. Alpha Gold clung on, howling.

Axel glanced over his shoulder. "Are those two fighting again?"

"IT SEEMS SO."

"Good. Let's lose them. I'm heading for the hills."

Alpha Gold screamed and yelled while his

brother laughed. All of a sudden, Alpha One felt pretty good about being the one to pilot the chopper.

"Thugeddigawaaaaaay!" bawled Alpha Gold.

"Sorry?" yelled Alpha One. "Say that again?"

"They're getting away!"

Alpha One looked up and saw that Axel and BEAST had swerved off course, and were now heading toward the hills. "Aw, no. If they get in among those craggy parts, we might lose them."

"So set me down already. No, wait! *Gently!*"

But Alpha One had already let the snowmobile go. It plunged down and landed on the ice with a jarring **crash.** Alpha Gold, apparently none the worse for wear, revved his engine and set off in pursuit.

Alpha One wasn't about to be left out of

the chase. He swiveled the searchlight until it clearly lit up SNOWDOG, then zoomed after the fleeing robot and its pilot.

Axel was running out of ideas. He'd hoped to thread in and out of the snowy hills until they lost sight of him, but with that chopper in the air he had no chance to hide. Maybe BEAST ought to shift form? He might be able to shoot the chopper down with **LAZBOLT,** but that form moved too slowly to be much use. **MYTHFIRE,** then? Axel decided no. He had no idea what MYTHFIRE even did, and the middle of a chase was no place to take random chances.

The only way out of here was to outrun them through sheer speed. "BEAST, give me all the power you've got."

"WARNING: BOOSTING ENGINE POWER BEYOND SAFE LIMITS WILL

DRAIN MY ENERGY CELLS."

"I know. We've got to. So do it."

A whining noise came from BEAST's insides. Axel smelled **burning.** SNOWDOG's engine roared louder than ever, and the caterpillar tracks whipped around and around, shooting them forward faster than a race car on the ice.

Axel looked back at the retreating figures of Alpha Gold on the ground and Alpha One in the air. They were losing them. It was all going to be okay. They were going to make it.

He looked ahead again … and that's when he saw **the crevasse.**

Pure horror gripped him. It was directly in their path, a **jagged crack** in the ice that looked as broad as the Grand Canyon.

There was no way around, and they were going too fast to stop …

CHAPTER 7

The crevasse gaped in front of them. In seconds, they would plunge into it. BEAST would be **smashed to bits** against the ice wall.

The caterpillar tracks spun. BEAST's engines screamed. Axel reached for the brake, then hesitated. Slowing down now would have no effect. They'd just skid over the edge no matter what he did. And there was no time to change forms to something that could fly.

Axel saw a small hump of piled-up snow at the chasm's edge, and a desperate plan came into his head. He squeezed the accelerator and steered BEAST toward it.

"ALERT! ALERT! HAZARD AHEAD!" BEAST warned him.

"I know."

"CHANCE OF AVOIDING HAZARD AT CURRENT SPEED: ZERO PERCENT."

"I'm not planning on avoiding it!"

Behind them, Alpha Gold was revving his own snowmobile as hard as he could. He followed right in their path, using the churned-up trench through the snow they'd left in their wake as a road. He grinned. "Target in sight. I'm closing in."

The snow mound grew larger in Axel's view. The treads ripped at the snow. He clenched the accelerator as hard as he could and prayed.

BEAST hit the mound and rushed up it as if it were a ramp. The next second, he shot over the edge and out across the crevasse. Axel felt a moment of weightlessness. His stomach rose into his mouth.

The far side of the crevasse loomed, solid as a brick wall.

Crump! BEAST crashed down on the far edge, not quite clearing the crevasse. Axel slammed against the safety cushions. His seat belt dug into his arms and legs. Dislodged snow and shattered ice went tumbling down.

For a horrendous second, they **seesawed** on the edge. SNOWDOG's caterpillar tracks **scrabbled** at the loose snow like a cat desperate to get out of a bath, sending white powdery spray behind them.

Then, just as it seemed they were going to fall back into the void, one of the spiky tracks caught hold of the ice and held. With a **deep ROAR,** SNOWDOG hauled itself out of the gulf. "Oh, man," gasped Axel. "Oh, **piranha poop.** On toast. That was too close."

Alpha Gold's eyes widened inside his crash helmet. He had only just caught sight of the crevasse, and his snowmobile suddenly seemed like a **puny little toy** compared with SNOWDOG.

"Get after him!" yelled Alpha One from the helicopter. "What are you waiting for, a written invitation?"

"There's a gap!" Alpha Gold howled.

"So? The kid jumped it, you can jump it, too! Or are you chicken?"

Alpha Gold snarled at that. "Nobody calls *me* chicken. Least of all *you*."

"Oh yeah?"

"Yeah. Watch this!"

He zoomed toward the same snow ramp that Axel had used. Unfortunately, now that BEAST had driven over it, it was much flatter than it had been. Alpha Gold did not notice this. He put his fist in the air.

"Yaaaaahooo!" he cried.

Still punching the air, he went coasting over the edge. He flew in a **majestic arc** out into space, then down into the yawning chasm. His whoop turned into a scream as he realized he wasn't going to make it.

"Bailing out! **Bailing out!"**

Axel, who by now was well away from the crevasse, heard the screams and winced. "Poor guy. I guess he didn't make it."

BOOM! ... OOM ... OOM ...

An explosion echoed up from the crevasse, confirming that Alpha Gold had, indeed, not made it.

BEAST's scanners beeped. "GRABBEM AGENT IS **STILL ALIVE.**"

"How do you know?"

"HIS OWN GRABBEM SUIT IS COMPATIBLE WITH MY SOFTWARE. I CAN SCAN HIS VITAL SIGNS. HE HAS **SURVIVED THE CRASH.**"

"Good. Guess his guardian angel was watching out for him."

The Alpha boys were a colossal pain. They'd tried to capture BEAST, and if they had succeeded, BEAST would have been dismantled. They were enemies. No doubt about that. But Axel was still glad Alpha Gold hadn't become **Alpha Splat.**

"How long until **the Devastator** is charged?" he asked.

"TWO HOURS AND FORTY-FIVE MINUTES. WE STILL HAVE TIME TO STOP IT."

A thought struck Axel. "Wait. Alpha Gold's going to **freeze** to death out here, isn't he?"

"WITH CERTAINTY."

Axel thought hard, sighed heavily and made up his mind. "I hate to say it, but we've got to help him. That helicopter can't fly down into the crevasse to get him, but we can."

He steered SNOWDOG in a full one-eighty and headed back toward the crevasse. Smoke from the destroyed snowmobile was drifting up from it.

When they reached the edge, Axel looked down. It was like squinting from the top of a skyscraper. There was the burning snowmobile, far beneath them, a glimmer of flame in the distant blue depths. And there, clinging to a ledge halfway down, was the pitiful figure of Alpha Gold.

"I can't believe I'm doing this," Axel muttered. "BEAST, shift to your normal form. We're heading down there after him."

He fired BEAST's foot jets, gently. Then he slowly lowered them down into the abyss.

Alpha Gold looked up at them and shivered in fright. "And I thought my luck couldn't get any worse," he wailed. **"The kid's coming to finish me off!"**

Flying as carefully as he could, Axel dropped down past the ice wall until he was alongside Alpha Gold. He reached out with BEAST's hand and gripped the struggling Grabbem agent by the waist.

"Out you come," he said. "Gently does it …"

BEAST's foot rockets **stuttered** and the robot dropped a few feet.

"BEAST, what was that?"

"POWER IS CRITICALLY LOW," BEAST said. "MY ENERGY CELLS ARE DRAINED."

Axel groaned. Of course – he'd burned them out turning SNOWDOG's engine up so high earlier. He had forgotten all about that.

"Sorry about this," he told Alpha Gold. Then he threw the man up and out of the chasm.

Alpha Gold sailed through the air in a **majestic arc** (again), only this time, he landed with a **whump** on the far side of the crevasse. He lay there spread-eagled in the snow, dizzy and confused, but crazily happy to be alive.

The helicopter flew down close to him. The spotlight lit him up.

"What are you playing at?" yelled Alpha One.

"I'm making a snow angel," giggled Alpha Gold, swishing his arms and legs in the snow. "And it sure is **pretty.**"

Meanwhile, BEAST dropped down another few feet. Axel quickly grabbed hold of a clump of ice that jutted out of the chasm wall. He shut off the foot jets to save what little power there was left.

From up above came the sound of Alpha One's helicopter passing by. Axel thought for one wild moment that the Grabbem agent might be coming to **help him,** to repay him for having saved his brother. Then the sound grew fainter as the helicopter flew away over the ice, taking Alpha Gold with it.

Axel sighed. *Typical Grabbem agents*, he thought. *They only look out for their own.*

BEAST had only a tiny sliver of power left. It didn't look like enough to fly them out of the chasm.

"Flying's too risky. We'll just have to climb out." Axel reached up and tried to dig BEAST's thick robotic fingers into the ice, to make a handhold.

The ice **shattered** in his powerful grasp. Suddenly he was holding on to nothing. BEAST's arms flailed as they fell backward.

"No!" Axel screamed, but it was too late.

They plunged down into the icy crevasse. BEAST **smashed** into one side then the other as they fell, shaking Axel around in his cockpit. It grew darker and darker as their long fall took them deep below the surface. Axel flung BEAST's arms and legs out, trying desperately to wedge them and stop their fall, but they were falling too fast for that.

A brutal **crash** ended their drop. BEAST lay pinned sideways in the narrow bottom of the crevasse. Axel looked up at the dim opening far above them.

"BEAST, are you okay?"

BEAST just made a noise like static. The text displays inside his head were gone, replaced with boxes full of meaningless snow.

"Oh, no. Please don't let this be the end. Come on, BEAST. Start up again." Axel held down BEAST's power button and prayed.

Instead of the soft ping of BEAST powering up, there was a sickly **thunk.** BEAST's whole inside compartment went dark. The whir of his fans, which kept Axel supplied with warm air, stopped dead.

It was funny how you didn't realize a noise was even there until it stopped.

Cold began to *creep* into BEAST's cockpit.

Axel told himself not to panic. He was trapped at the bottom of an icy ravine inside a robot that wasn't working, and soon he would freeze to death. But if he panicked, it would be even worse. He'd just start screaming and never stop. He breathed slowly in and out and forced himself to think clearly.

That was when the **cave-in** happened.

First it was just a few shards of ice falling down the chasm, from where BEAST's crash descent had knocked them loose. Then a rush of snow followed, then fat boulders of solid ice, tumbling and roaring down to where BEAST lay motionless.

WHOOSH!

It was like being under a mixer pouring out gravelly concrete. Axel could only watch, helpless, as tons of Antarctic ice buried him alive …

CHAPTER 8

Silence.

Axel lay in total darkness, listening to nothing. The silence was even worse than the noise had been. At least the noise had meant they were still part of the real world. But now, in this never-ending darkness, they might as well be in starless space.

His feet were growing cold now. He tried not to think about what that meant.

He thought about his mother back at home, who had tried to feed him a hot meal before he rushed off. Then Axel bit his lip so he wouldn't start crying. If only BEAST had a time-travel app ... Axel would head back in time and do it all differently this time around.

"I'm hungry," he said hoarsely to himself.

Something deep inside BEAST made a strange **grinding** noise.

Axel hesitated. Was that just the sound of the heavy ice crushing BEAST out of shape? Or had there been a flicker of life from his friend?

"I'm hungry," he repeated, and listened hard.

BEAST *buzzed*, low and long. He made a strangled-sounding beep. His display screens flared into life, then showed nothing but a single blinking dot.

LIQUI-NUMS!™

"When there's no time for taste!"

"LI. LI. LI," said BEAST. "LICK. LIQUI. **LIQUI-NUMS.**" The fans began to hum, and a soft warm breeze flowed into the cockpit. **"LIQUI-NUMS ARE AVAILABLE.** EMERGENCY LIFE SUPPORT ACTIVE."

"You're alive!" Axel nearly cried with relief. He almost felt like drinking some of the disgusting **Liqui-Nums** just to show BEAST how glad he was to have him back.

"YES, AXEL. MY PILOT NEEDED ME."

"But I thought your energy cells were all used up!"

"BEAST CREATED AN **EMERGENCY BACKUP CELL** EARLIER ON," said BEAST. "IT WAS THE SEAL'S IDEA."

Axel stared in total confusion. "The leopard seal?"

"YES. SHE TOLD ME SOMETHING IMPORTANT."

BEAST paused, and Axel wondered if he was deciding whether to tell him or not.

"SHE SAID: THE SMALL ONE INSIDE YOU IS **YOUR RESPONSIBILITY.** YOU MUST MAKE SURE HE EATS."

"Make sure he eats," Axel echoed.

"BEAST MAY USE ENERGY FOR OTHER THINGS, BUT BEAST MUST ALWAYS KEEP ENOUGH TO LOOK AFTER HIS PILOT, BECAUSE HIS PILOT **DOES NOT ALWAYS LOOK AFTER HIMSELF.**"

"You're right," Axel said. "I don't. And I'm sorry." He took a deep breath. "I handled this all wrong. I know that now. I wanted to go off on a mission so bad, I just rushed off recklessly without taking any time to plan. Or even eat."

"LIQUI-NUMS ARE AVAILABLE," BEAST insisted.

"Fine. I'll have some."

The drinking straw reappeared. Axel made a face and took a slurp. It was still revolting, but it was better than nothing. *Next time*, he thought, *I won't rush blindly into things*.

If there even **was** a next time. BEAST was awake again, but they were still trapped under ice at the bottom of a ravine.

Axel tried to move BEAST's arms and legs, but he could do barely more than wiggle them a few inches. Shifting to **OGRE** form might have helped – OGRE was strong enough to lift trucks – but they didn't have that app loaded.

Once again, Axel wished he had one of his mother's hot meals inside him right now.

"Heat," he whispered. "Maybe that's the answer." He checked the list of loaded apps, and one stood out. "BEAST, can you shift to **MYTHFIRE** form?"

"YES."

"Do it. It's time to find out what it does."

BEAST's body shifted shape a little. Axel heard armor plates grind and lock into place. Claws extended from BEAST's fingers. His head extended, growing out until it looked like a robotic crocodile, or maybe a dinosaur.

It was suddenly a lot **warmer** inside BEAST. Some new weapons options lit up:

- **claw strike**
- **tail strike**
- **fire armor**
- **flame blast**

Axel stared at **flame blast** and all at once he understood.

He fired the flame blast. Two scorching jets of fire billowed out from MYTHFIRE's nostrils. They seared right through the ice, melting it away in seconds. Water hissed and boiled away as steam.

MYTHFIRE wasn't a crocodile, and he wasn't a dinosaur.

MYTHFIRE was a **dragon!**

Axel hit **fire armor.** He pulled one of BEAST's now-clawed hands free and saw that it was glowing red.

MYTHFIRE's whole body was becoming scorching hot. The ice shrank and melted away at its touch like butter.

Axel swiped and raked the ice, clambering out of the widening crater. They looked like some mythical monster from a forgotten era of history, trapped for untold centuries under the frozen crust, now breaking free at long last.

Soon MYTHFIRE stood fully revealed, **glowing bright red** in the darkness. There was still a chasm stretching above them, but they were free. They could move again. There was still hope.

Just as Axel was thinking their luck had finally changed, he heard something that sent his spirits crashing again. Voices were yelling to one another from the top of the crevasse:

"This is where they fell, I know it!"

"What's that light? Is it them?"

"Something's **on fire** down there. You think the robot wrecked itself?"

"Nah, it's too tough. Keep watching. We're going to be the ones to claim that reward, boys."

Axel groaned. Grabbem agents – dozens of them, by the sound of it. Alpha One and Alpha Gold must have alerted the base, and now a whole detachment of Grabbem agents was out here to take them prisoner. There was a fat reward for bringing BEAST back to the corporation that had built him.

"We've got to get out of here," Axel told BEAST.

"AGREED," said BEAST.

"Can we climb out?"

"YES, BUT THERE ARE NOW MANY GRABBEM AGENTS WAITING FOR US UP THERE. OUR CHANCES OF ESCAPE ARE **ZERO POINT ZERO ZERO TWO PERCENT.**"

"Oh, fantastic!" This whole mission was going from bad to worse. He angrily thrust MYTHFIRE's glowing fist into the icy wall, and watched in grim satisfaction as the ice water **seethed and bubbled** around it.

Then, more thoughtfully, he drew the fist out. There was a smooth, wide hollow left behind.

He grinned. "You know, BEAST, maybe we don't need to get out after all …"

CHAPTER 9

MYTHFIRE's red-hot armor had probably been meant for combat, Axel guessed. An enemy would think twice about grabbing a robot that was hot enough to cause serious damage.

Melting escape tunnels through solid ice — like they were doing now — was just a bonus.

"How long until **the Devastator** is due to appear?" Axel asked.

"TWENTY MINUTES."

Axel gritted his teeth. They were almost out of time already. SNOWDOG would have made it to the base far more quickly.

MYTHFIRE took stride after stride, blasting ahead with its **fiery breath** and using its glowing hands and feet to melt the ice in its path. BEAST's reserve cell was steadily running out of power. Axel hoped they'd reach the base soon.

He thought of the Grabbem agents who were waiting in the cold at the edge of the crevasse, still thinking that he and BEAST were bound to come climbing out sooner or later. They'd be waiting a long, long time …

"I AM DETECTING LARGE AMOUNTS OF METAL UP AHEAD," announced BEAST suddenly.

"That's got to be the base!"

Sure enough, a gray metallic surface soon showed through the ice. Axel cleared away a large enough patch to enter through and gave the metal an experimental **tap.**

"Sounds solid. Let's look for a way in."

But there was no door, not in that spot, nor anywhere nearby. The wall seemed to be made of great steel plates like the hull of a battleship.

"Okay, so we *make* a way in!" Axel scraped MYTHFIRE's claws across the metal, but the only result was a ghastly *screeching* sound and a few faint scratches.

"I RECOMMEND **LAZBOLT**," said BEAST.

Axel had tried LAZBOLT only once before, and that had been after dark in the backyard at home. Shortly after their first adventure together, Agent Omega had sent them some experimental apps to test out, including LAZBOLT.

When he discovered that LAZBOLT was an incredibly powerful **laser-beam cannon,** Axel had gotten it into his head that it might be possible to carve his initials on the moon and BEAST did not think to warn him that this was not a good idea. Their first attempt at laser-assisted planetoid vandalism lasted only a millisecond, lit up the countryside for miles around with **shocking green light,** and resulted in Axel being banned from video games for a week as punishment. Nedra had blamed the strange light on "fireworks," which had seemed to satisfy the neighbors.

BEAST now understood that the moon was part of the natural world, as much so as the trees and flowers he loved, and refused to allow Axel to fire energy beams at it for any reason.

"Have you got enough power left?"

"ENOUGH FOR ONE SIXTY-SECOND BLAST."

BEAST shifted form. MYTHFIRE's claws and snout vanished away. BEAST's legs retracted, and a trundling platform took their place. From his back emerged a thick needle-tipped prong on the end of an angled strut. A delicate-looking bloom of silvery metal fanned out around it, like a satellite dish. This was **LAZBOLT's** beam projector.

Axel fired. A streak of light too bright to look at erupted from the projector and hit the wall. The metal instantly began to **sizzle** and melt.

Carefully, Axel moved the beam in an oval, slicing through the wall. *I hope this isn't a gas or oil pipe*, he thought. *We'd be blown to bits.*

Fifty-three seconds later, LAZBOLT's energy beam finished cutting and switched off. The cutout piece of wall fell inward with a heavy **CLANG.**

Axel waited for a moment, in case any guards appeared. But there was only silence.

Axel shifted BEAST back into his regular form. Cautiously, they stepped inside and entered the Grabbem base.

The base was made from a **hollowed-out iceberg.** From outside, it would look just like part of the Antarctic landscape. Inside, it was a very different story. The first thing you noticed was the enormous pit in the middle of the base. It gave Axel a creepy feeling as he peered at it. He felt sure there was something down there, something sinister.

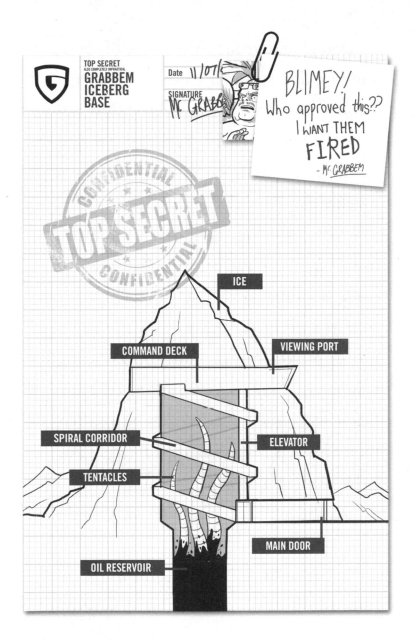

Around and around the inside of the base, winding in a spiral from bottom to top like a corkscrew, was a metal tube with windows in it. This was where Axel and Beast were standing now. Orange lights lit the tube with a sickly glow.

Around the central pit was a cluster of metal platforms and catwalks, like scaffolding on a building site. Power cables dangled from the struts like spaghetti. Little bug-eyed robots patrolled back and forth, tapping on computer terminals and working on pieces of machinery. Axel guessed they were there to look after whatever was down in that pit.

He had to know what was in there. To do that he had to get a better view, and that meant climbing higher up.

He drove BEAST up several levels of the tubular corridor until he could look down into the pit. "BEAST, zoom in," he said.

He caught his breath as he saw what was lurking in the icy shadows. "Oh, man," he said. "So *that's* what they're up to!"

The thing lurking in the central pit was, in fact, several things: a group of **fat metallic tentacles** as wide around as express trains. They squirmed and stretched upward hungrily.

Their pointed tips held sawlike clusters of teeth. In the middle of the teeth were gaping holes like puckered mouths. It was like looking at a hideous **animatronic monster octopus.**

The tentacles moved as if they were alive, reaching up toward the light and **wavering** from side to side as if they smelled something. One of them had black, gooey stuff all over its mouth. The way they moved made Axel feel queasy. They reminded him of **leeches** hungry for blood.

That's exactly what they are, he thought. *Only it's the blood of the Earth they want to suck up.*

"They want oil," said Axel. "Those things are oil pipes. With teeth!"

Was *this* the Devastator, he wondered? *No, it couldn't be.* Agent Omega had said the Devastator was a vehicle. These things must be **waiting** for the Devastator to blast holes through the ice sheet. Then they could feast on the rich oil underneath.

"FIVE MINUTES REMAINING," said BEAST …

CHAPTER 10

"We've got to find **the Devastator** and shut it down," Axel said. "And I don't even know what it looks like!"

The little robots on the walkways around the pit hadn't noticed him peering in. Axel looked around, but he couldn't see a single human being anywhere. Maybe the humans were holed up somewhere safe and warm while the robots did all the work.

Most of the robots were busy on the walkways. There didn't seem to be any inside the tubular corridor at all. With any luck, Axel could explore a little way and not get caught. But he couldn't stomp around inside BEAST without being noticed. He'd have to go alone.

He popped open BEAST's hatch and climbed out. "I'm going to go look for the Devastator," he said, his teeth **chattering.**

"WAIT," said BEAST. The robot opened a hatch in his own leg and pulled out a heavy parka. "BEAST CAN TOLERATE THE COLD. AXEL CANNOT."

Axel gratefully fastened the fur-lined coat around himself. "It's perfect! Where did you find this?"

"BEAST PACKED IT FOR YOU."

"Thanks! Hey, isn't that a power outlet?

Why don't you plug in and recharge your energy cells? I'll scout ahead."

BEAST unspooled a cable from his finger, plugged himself in and gave a contented sigh. His dim eyes began to shine brightly again.

Axel ran up the metal corridor. He passed heavy bulkhead doors and wall-mounted gun turrets that rotated to follow him. A sign in blue and yellow pointed the way upward to the *Command Deck*. That sounded promising.

It turned out to be at the very top of the base, and Axel was out of breath by the time he reached it. He grimaced as he noticed an open-sided elevator nearby. *If I'd known that was there, I wouldn't have needed to run all the way up here!*

The Command Deck was a room full of computer screens and huge windows that looked out over the snowy wasteland. White metal shutters had previously hidden the windows from outside view, but now they had been rolled back.

On one of the screens was a countdown: **D MINUS 10.** Axel didn't have to guess what the **D** stood for. He desperately looked for some way to shut it down.

"What are you doing in here, human?" said a twangy electronic voice.

Axel spun around. One of the little robots was standing in the doorway, looking at him with big, round, accusing eyes.

"Um, maintenance?"

"Maintenance?" said the robot, as if Axel had said he was here to do some ballet dancing. **"You're supposed to be out with the rest of the human agents! Didn't you hear the full alert?"**

"Must have, ah, missed it," Axel said and

grabbed the sides of his hood. "These furry hoods sure do muffle sounds, yes they do."

The computer flashed up **D MINUS 9.**

Axel began tapping keys at random, trying to find some way to stop it. "Do you mind?" he told the robot. "Got lots of work to do."

The robot didn't have eyebrows, but if it had it would have furrowed them. **"What's your Grabbem ID number?"** it said menacingly.

"It's classified," Axel said. He was beginning to wish he'd picked a room with more than one exit. "Can't tell you."

The robot hummed toward him. **"Classified? Are you trying to tell me you're with Special Ops?"**

"Yes! Special Ops, that's me. We're doing something very secret."

"More secret than this entire

secret base, I suppose?"

Axel hadn't known a robot could sound sarcastic. Meanwhile, the computer screen flicked over to **D MINUS 8.**

Something large and green loomed behind the robot. It was BEAST, all finished with recharging. He bent down and stared in through the door. His shining eyes went big with alarm as he saw Axel's panicked face.

The little robot hadn't noticed BEAST.

"I don't think you're Special Ops at all," it said. **"Your story doesn't add up. Wait. I know what's going on!"** It jiggled excitedly. **"There's a renegade Grabbem droid here somewhere, and it can change its shape."**

"Wow. Imagine that," said Axel, looking right at BEAST.

"I think maybe the renegade droid

is right here, and I'm looking at him!" declared the robot triumphantly.

Axel stared in amazement. Did the robot really think … that *he* was …

"You're going to have to come with me," said the robot. It lifted two tiny arms. Axel was about to burst out laughing, because they looked about as menacing as egg whisks, but then a blue arc of electricity **crackled** between them.

He began to back away.

"Don't worry," the robot said. **"It's just an electron pulse. To disable your circuits."**

Fizz, crackle went the energy current.

Axel knew perfectly well that he didn't have any circuits, but an electric jolt wouldn't do him any good either. He backed away farther and almost tripped over a steel trash can.

"It was clever to disguise yourself as a human, but you could never fool a top-of-the-line Grabbem office robot!"

Axel pointed. "Watch out, it's a giant robot penguin!"

The robot spun its head around without moving the rest of its body. It saw BEAST filling the doorway. It made a terrified buzzing noise that sounded like a frog croaking through aluminum foil.

"QUACK," said BEAST.

Axel quickly grabbed the trash can and slammed it down over the robot's head.

Blinded, the robot careered around the Command Deck knocking things over.

"Alert! Alert!" it shouted. **"Renegade droid! Base invasion! Alert –"**

BEAST bashed his fist down on top of the metal trash can, crumpling it. The robot grabbed the trash can with its flimsy arms, which were still sizzling with the stored-up pulse.

There was a *flash* and a **BANG.**

The robot stood perfectly still. Smoke began to curl out of its arm sockets and from under the squashed trash can.

"I think he just fried his own brain," Axel said.

The computer flashed up: **D MINUS 1. DEPLOYMENT COMPLETE.**

"TIME IS UP," said BEAST.

"What?"

"THE DEVASTATOR IS LAUNCHING."

Suddenly a booming voice rang out from hidden loudspeakers echoing all across the base.

"Attention, all loyal Grabbem employees! This is your beloved CEO's son, Gus Grabbem

Junior, speaking. It gives me great pleasure to declare this Antarctic **oil drilling** operation **OPEN!**"

Down below them in the base, the robots stopped what they were doing, raised their little arms and cheered. And at that moment, **the Devastator appeared.**

It strode out from a side tunnel that Axel hadn't even noticed, and walked past the gaping pit where the tentacles writhed and chomped.

In the front of the hollow iceberg, a gigantic hidden door opened. The Devastator **stomped** through it and out into the Antarctic wilderness.

"Now it's time to punch the first hole of many to come," said Gus Grabbem Junior. **"Hold on to your hats,** people!"

"We're too late," Axel said. "The penguins, the seals, the fish … we can't save them. Grabbem are going to trash the whole ecosystem now!"

CHAPTER

11

The Devastator went stomping out of the base. Axel and BEAST could see it clearly through the Command Deck windows. It stalked across the snow on its three spindly legs, then stopped suddenly.

"First drill point reached. Time to unleash some rage!" roared Gus, and punched a button.

A searing beam shot down from the middle of the Devastator. It speared through the ice, sending up huge clouds of steam. The light from the beam shone through the billowing clouds. It made the Devastator look like a horrifying demon, perched on a throne of smoke and fire.

Gus laughed in delight. **"Oh, yeah. Feel the burn."**

Axel had a sick, wrong feeling in his stomach. Gus was just a boy, not much older than he was. The power of that beam was … well, **devastating.** He shouldn't have been entrusted with it. It was like giving a submachine gun to a baby.

The Devastator stepped backward, away from the steaming hole it had left in the ice.

The next moment, inside the base, the biggest of the tentacles **lunged** upward out of the pit. It charged through the open door of the base and kept on going.

It extended out from the base, stretching farther and farther over the ice until it neared the freshly bored hole. Then it seemed to speed up, as if it were excited. It wriggled down into the hole, making a **churning, grinding noise.** The fat tentacle began to squirm and flex as it dug down to the oil.

"We've got to stop that thing, fast," yelled Axel. "BEAST, shift into **LAZBOLT** form and follow me!"

BEAST *whizzed* along behind Axel as he sprinted out of the Command Deck. Running all the way around and around the spiral tube to the ground floor would take too long, so he headed for the open-sided elevator that would take them straight down to the ground.

As he ran, he saw that more of the tentacles were rearing up. It was **feeding time.**

BEAST headed onto the elevator platform. Axel shoved the lever down to the **"ground floor"** setting and quickly climbed inside BEAST.

As the elevator began to sink, Axel carefully aimed LAZBOLT's cannon at the main tentacle.

"Mealtime's over," he growled, and fired.

LAZBOLT's beam sliced clean through the tentacle before the oil had even begun to flow. The severed stump thrashed around. The grinding machinery sounded like screams.

The whole base went crazy. Sirens **blared** and emergency lights *flashed.* The robots dashed around in a panic, some trying to reach the exits, others trying to reach Axel. They **collided** with one another in their confusion. A few unlucky ones were knocked off the edge of the walkway and fell howling into the darkness.

Axel forced himself to concentrate. He let off shot after shot, each one neatly slicing through a rampaging tentacle. The elevator continued its **all-too-slow** descent toward the ground floor.

A group of robots crowded at the end of a walkway, ready to swarm onto the elevator the moment it reached them. Axel quickly used LAZBOLT to cut away the supports. With a groaning noise of overloaded metal, the walkway bent under the robots' weight. **Bleeping and jostling,** the robots tried to fight their way off again, but the walkway bent in half and the crowd went tumbling off the edge.

His heart hammering, Axel severed tentacle after tentacle until only one was left.

The snaking metal thing hesitated and turned to face him.

"IT SMELLS MY OIL," BEAST said. His voice quavered. **"HELP, AXEL. HELP."**

Axel tried to fire. The control wouldn't respond.

The tentacle reared up above the platform.

Axel saw that LAZBOLT wasn't locked on to it like it should be. He tried to fire, but the LAZBOLT control just clicked without doing anything. He tried to move BEAST's arms. They wouldn't budge. "BEAST, snap out of it!" Axel shouted. *"Fire!"*

Nothing happened.

The tentacle opened its mouth wide, revealing all the **grinding** circular teeth within.

He's scared, Axel thought. *Oil must be like blood to robots. Fear is locking him up completely, like a rabbit in the headlights. He's too scared to move!*

As calmly as he could, Axel said, "BEAST, you can take this thing. Just remember how awesome you are."

"BEAST IS FRIGHTENED!"

"I know. It's okay. **You can do this.** Believe in yourself!"

The tentacle rushed at them.

BEAST **fired** the LAZBOLT cannon right into the cavernous mouth. The bolt ripped along the tentacle's length and **exploded** out of its side. It fell back, belching smoke, **whipping** from side to side. BEAST fired again and again until only mangled, glowing metal showed through the smoke.

As the ravaged tentacle finally stopped thrashing, the elevator came to a stop beside the pit. The main base doors were dead ahead.

"You okay?" Axel asked gently.

"BEAST IS FINE."

"Good."

"BEAST DID IT!"

Axel smiled. "Yes, you did. Good going, BEAST. Now it's time to take care of the Devastator."

He hit the throttle, and they **zoooomed** out onto the ice.

Gus Grabbem Junior had been hard at work. He clearly didn't know the tentacles had all been knocked out, because six or seven freshly bored holes were now smoking in the ice sheet. He caught sight of BEAST and came stomping over to meet them, carried on the Devastator's long stalking legs.

"Hey!" Gus's amplified voice boomed out. **"You there. Why aren't the other tentacles coming out?"**

"He hasn't recognized us," Axel whispered. "We just need one good zap, and that Devastator is toast. Aim for the legs."

LAZBOLT took aim.

But Gus hadn't spent all those hours playing video games without learning a thing or two. Some instinct inside his brutal mind warned him there was danger ahead. He wrenched the Devastator sideways, sending it staggering across the ice just as LAZBOLT's beam zipped through the air.

"You!" Gus hissed. **"The kid who stole my robot** – and tricked me into thinking I'd **blown it up!"**

"Keep talking," said Axel, thinking: *and I'll keep aiming.*

"I should have known you were still out there. Fine. I'll just have to **finish you off** myself."

Axel tried to lock on again, but Gus was wise to him. The Devastator was nimble for such a huge vehicle, and the spindly legs moved as quickly as a spider's. Gus weaved left and right, dodging LAZBOLT's beams, and in seconds he was squatting directly above them.

"Move!" Axel yelled. He tried to drive BEAST out of the way, but LAZBOLT's trundling platform wasn't built for speed.

Light shone in through the cockpit canopy as the Devastator's beam warmed up ...

CHAPTER 12

"BEAST, change form! Go into **SNOWDOG!**"

The light from the Devastator grew blinding as BEAST shifted his shape. The second that SNOWDOG was ready, Axel hit the throttle as hard as it would go.

SNOWDOG roared out from under the Devastator. The intense beam **blazed** down right where they'd just been, turning it into a molten pit.

"Get back here, you chicken!"

yelled Gus. He gave chase.

Axel and BEAST went roaring over the snow. The Devastator was striding after them, and it was catching up fast. "We need to shift into SKYHAWK and out of here," Axel said. "But if we shift out of SNOWDOG, we'll stop moving and we'll be sitting ducks!"

He put on speed, but the Devastator was still gaining on them. Any moment now it would be towering right above them again, ready to let loose another blast. They couldn't outrun it forever. Right on cue, the Devastator's middle leg **stomped** down directly in their path.

Axel looked up and saw a terrifying sight: the Devastator's blaster, **fully charged**, shimmering with heat, about to burn him to a crisp. He let out a yell and swung SNOWDOG around in a curve so tight that one set of treads lifted clean off the ground. As the deadly beam lashed down, SNOWDOG's treads churned the snow and they scooted away from the Devastator again.

"I can **do this** all day," shouted Gus Grabbem. "I'm not **tired** yet!"

All Axel could think to do was keep on driving. He skidded in **wild turns** and drove between craggy ice formations, hoping the Devastator wouldn't be able to follow. But the fearsome machine was well designed. The Devastator went clambering up rocky hills and skittering across valleys, all without losing any speed at all.

"We need a plan, BEAST," Axel panted, as they dodged yet another scorching blast from above. "How can we lose him?"

"I DO NOT KNOW. HE IS FASTER AND HIS WEAPON IS MORE POWERFUL."

"What about the crevasse? We could jump it again."

"THE DEVASTATOR CAN SIMPLY STEP OVER IT."

"Oh, geez. I didn't even think of that … **whoa!**"

Axel swerved to avoid a pit in the ice ahead of them. It dawned on him that the Devastator had made that pit only moments before. They must have played this **cat-and-mouse** game for so long that they'd doubled back on themselves! They were on the flat ice plain again, only it was more dangerous than ever now that Gus had shot holes in it.

"He doesn't have a plan either," Axel muttered. "He's just **blasting away** with that cannon of his! Totally reckless …"

He reminds me of someone, Axel thought. **Me.** *He's thinking in the moment instead of* *planning ahead. That's the same mistake I made before.* "I wonder," he mused. "BEAST, I've got an idea."

From his seat high up in the Devastator, Gus saw SNOWDOG suddenly change course. Instead of weaving wildly around trying to dodge him, the robot went zooming out toward the shore.

"Making a break for it, eh?" Gus grinned. **"Where** are you going to go?"

Axel glanced back. Gus was sprinting after them, just like he was supposed to. Now for the dangerous part.

SNOWDOG *charged* down the slope toward the level shelf of ice that lay on the water. It stretched out to sea for almost half a mile. Axel blasted the horn to warn any real penguins or seals to get out of the way.

They plowed through the snow and out onto the marine ice. Just before they reached the very limit, Axel hit the brakes. SNOWDOG **skidded** to a stop at the ice's edge. They were surrounded by the Antarctic sea on three sides. Loose floes bobbed around in the water beyond, rocking gently.

Gus guffawed. **"Hah!** Now you're **trapped!"**

The Devastator strode out onto the ice shelf where SNOWDOG sat motionless. It quickly closed the distance. Axel watched BEAST's rear-view screen as the three towering metal legs came down around him. The ice below them groaned, but didn't give.

"Feel the burn," snarled Gus.

Almost, thought Axel as the Devastator's underside began to glow. *Almost* ... **NOW!**

He slammed SNOWDOG into full reverse.

SNOWDOG shot backward just as the Devastator's beam lashed down.

Steam rose. Ice melted to vapor instantly. A widening crater opened up – and then, with a thunderous crash, the ice shelf **shattered.**

Axel had been counting on that. In his eagerness to blast them to ashes, Gus had forgotten that the marine ice was only a few feet thick. Underneath it was the cold, deep Antarctic sea.

The Devastator was suddenly standing on a group of floating ice floes, and it couldn't balance. It **wobbled** like a flamingo on roller skates, tilted sideways and fell.

Water flew up in a giant wave as the huge saucer body **plunged** into the sea.

"No!" Gus screamed through the transparent bubble. **"This thing can't swim. Get back here, you ... arrrr!"**

Gradually, the Devastator sank below the surface, taking Gus Grabbem Junior with it. Axel watched the glowing shape disappear. Above the spot where the Devastator had vanished, fragments of ice drifted lazily around.

"He'll be okay, won't he?" Axel asked BEAST.

BEAST made calculating noises. "HE WILL SURVIVE FOR AT LEAST TWENTY-FOUR HOURS."

"Good. Plenty of time for someone to rescue him."

"WE COULD RESCUE HIM OURSELVES," BEAST said.

"I've got a better idea. Remember that trawler we saw earlier? Let's send them a message ..."

Many hours later, Axel sat at the table in his own house, opposite BEAST. A huge plate of food lay in front of him, and the electric heater was turned up to high. Nedra and Rosie sat with him, but nobody was eating yet. They were all watching the little TV in the corner of the room.

On the TV, a news team was reporting the astonishing rescue of Gus Grabbem Junior, heir to the **multi-bulti-billion-dollar** Grabbem fortune, from a mysterious wreck in the Antarctic. The footage showed happy Chinese fishermen hoisting a soaking-wet Gus aboard their boat while he scowled at the camera.

Heroes of the sea, read the caption. *Teenager's rescue "a miracle," claims mother.*

"Grabbem Industries had repeatedly denied rumors that they had a presence in the Antarctic," said the newscaster. "However, they have now admitted setting up a 'research base,' which they also claim has been destroyed in a **freak accident.** Grabbem's share prices have dropped sharply at the news, and questions will surely be raised at the next United Nations summit."

"I didn't need rescuing!" Gus shouted at the camera. "I had it all under control. Turn those cameras off!"

Back in the studio, the newscaster straightened her papers. "This program approached Gus Grabbem Senior, head of the corporation, for comment. He has no, er, *comment* to make at this time."

The newscaster's smile suddenly disappeared. She lowered her glasses and looked right at the camera. "And on a personal note, I would just like to add that there was no call for him to use such **disgusting** language, especially when addressing a well-respected reporter. Money cannot buy everything, and in Mr. Grabbem's case, it clearly **cannot** buy good manners. Shame on you, sir."

Axel's mouth fell open.

The newscaster's bright smile reappeared. "This has been Maisie Penderby, Channel 99 News. Here's Jim with the weather."

Bit by bit, we're chipping away at Grabbem, Axel thought. *One day, the whole world will know how bad they really are.*

Nedra switched the TV off. "Looks like you two did a good job out there," she said distantly.

"I guess." Axel fidgeted. "Mom ... I'm sorry."

"Sorry!" she burst out. "I should think you're sorry, after what you did! Don't ever run out of this house like that again, do you hear me?"

"I won't," said Axel, meaning it. "I promise."

To his surprise, she softened. "I know. Now listen." She moved her chair closer to his. "After you went shooting off, Agent Omega came back online and we had a little chat. He wanted to say sorry, too."

Axel blinked. **"What for?"**

"Because he felt responsible for what you did. He's enough of a man to take his share of the blame. And he's right to." She took a breath. "You and BEAST, you **need** to get out. You **need** to train together. If he hadn't demanded you both stay shut up in here, maybe you wouldn't have been so crazy desperate to rush off!"

"So does that mean we can go out and practice?"

Nedra nodded to Rosie, who said, "Your mom and I decided you can use my junkyard for **battle training.** Plenty of junk to use for target practice, and Grabbem won't show their faces there after what happened last time. Omega's fine with it, too. Sound good to you?"

"Sounds awesome." Axel grinned.

"**AWESOME,**" agreed BEAST.

"Right," Nedra declared. "Enough talk. Time for food."

"Smells good," said Rosie. "What is it?"

"Fish."

Axel laughed. "You just made a **leopard seal** very happy."

"What?"

"Never mind. Let's eat!"

THE END
(for now)

ABOUT THE AUTHOR
& ILLUSTRATOR

ADRIAN C. BOTT is a gamer, writer and professional adventure-creator. He lives in Sussex, England, with his family and is allowed to play video games whenever he wants.

ANDY ISAAC lives in Melbourne, Australia. He discovered his love of illustration through comic books when he  was eight years old, and has been creating his own characters ever since.